# RACHEL ISADORA

# I JUST WANT TO SAY GOOD NIGHT

 Nancy Paulsen Books

NANCY PAULSEN BOOKS
an imprint of Penguin Random House LLC
375 Hudson Street
New York, NY 10014

Library of Congress Cataloging-in-Publication Data
Names: Isadora, Rachel, author, illustrator. Title: I just want to say good night / Rachel Isadora.
Description: New York, NY : Nancy Paulsen Books, [2017]
Summary: In a village on the African plains, a little girl stalls bedtime
by saying good night to various animals and objects.
Identifiers: LCCN 2016014083 | ISBN 9780399173844 (hardback)
Subjects: | CYAC: Bedtime—Fiction. | Blacks—Africa—Fiction. | Africa—Fiction. |
BISAC: JUVENILE FICTION / Bedtime & Dreams. |
JUVENILE FICTION / People & Places / Africa. | JUVENILE FICTION
/ Health & Daily Living / Daily Activities.
Classification: LCC PZ7.1763 Ial 2017 | DDC [E]—dc23
LC record available at https://lccn.loc.gov/2016014083

Manufactured in China by RR Donnelley Asia Printing Solutions Ltd.

ISBN 9780399173844
Special Markets ISBN 9780525517191 Not for Resale
3  5  7  9  10  8  6  4  2

Design by Marikka Tamura.
Text set in Atelier Sans ITC Std.
The art was done in oil paint and ink.

To a great artist,
Uncle Joe Lasker

On the African veld, there is a village.
As the sun sets, parents tell their children,
"It is time for bed."

Lala greets her papa, who has been fishing.

"Ooh! You caught a big one!" she says.

"Yes, it was a good day," Papa says.

"It is time for bed,"
Papa tells Lala.

"I just want to say
good night to
the fish," Lala says.

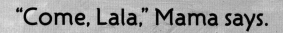

"Come, Lala," Mama says.

"I just want to say
good night to
the cat," Lala says.

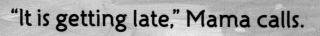

"It is getting late," Mama calls.

"I just want to say
good night to
the bird," Lala says.

"Lala!"

"I just want to say good night
to the goat," Lala says.

"It is time to go to sleep!" Mama calls.

"I just want to say good night
to the monkey," Lala says.

"Come *now*!"
Mama says.

"I just want to say good night to the chickens," Lala says.

"Oh, Lala!" Mama says.

"I just want to say good night
to the little ants," Lala says.

"I'm just not ready to go to sleep,"
Lala says to her dog.

"Now!" Mama says.

"Yes. Yes. I am coming.
I just want to say good night
to the rock," Lala says.

Lala gets into bed.
"Sweet dreams," Mama says.

"Good night,
Mama!"

"I just want to say good night to my book," Lala says.

"Good night, moon!"
she whispers and smiles.